STRIKE!

ROB CHILDS

Illustrated by Martin Chatterton

Perfect for new readers

STRIKE!
A CORGI PUPS BOOK 0552 550310

Published in Great Britain by Corgi Pups Books,
an imprint of Random House Children's Books

This edition published 2004

5 7 9 10 8 6 4

Papers used by Random House Children's Books are natural,
recyclable products made from wood grown in sustainable forests.
The manufacturing processes conform to the environmental regulations
of the country of origin.

Typeset in 18/25pt Bembo MT Schoolbook by
Palimpsest Book Production Limited,
Polmont, Stirlingshire

Corgi Books are published by Random House Children's Books,
61–63 Uxbridge Road, London W5 5SA,
a division of The Random House Group Ltd,
in Australia by Random House Australia (Pty) Ltd,
20 Alfred Street, Milsons Point, Sydney, NSW 2061, Australia,
in New Zealand by Random House New Zealand Ltd,
18 Poland Road, Glenfield, Auckland 10, New Zealand,
and in South Africa by Random House (Pty) Ltd,
Endulini, 5A Jubilee Road, Parktown 2193, South Africa

THE RANDOM HOUSE GROUP Limited Reg. No. 954009
www.kidsatrandomhouse.co.uk

A CIP catalogue record for this book
is available from the British Library.

Printed and bound in Great Britain by
Cox & Wyman Ltd, Reading, Berkshire

Contents

Series Reading Consultant: Prue Goodwin,
Lecturer in Literacy and Children's Books,
University of Reading

Chapter One
Adam Says

"Missed!"

"So?" Jake snorted, giving his younger brother a dirty look. "Can't catch one every time."

"You *never* catch one!" Owen
laughed. "Your mate Adam says
you always strike too early."

Jake reeled in the line and
took another worm out of his
bait tin. "Better too early than
too late," he muttered.

"And Adam says—"

Jake cut him off. "Adam doesn't even *go* fishing."

"That's because he thinks it's cruel. He says the fish get hurt . . ."

Jake took a step up the bank towards him and Owen moved smartly away out of reach.

"You'll get hurt in a minute,"
Jake warned. "I'll chuck you in
the brook so you can ask the
fish what *they* think!"

Owen kept at a safe distance
– just in case. He waited until
his brother had made his next
cast before he spoke again.

"It's the same in football."

"What is?"

"The way you keep missing."

"Rubbish!"

"Oh yeah? So how many goals have you scored for Rangers?"

Jake gave what he hoped was a casual shrug. "Dunno," he mumbled. "Not really been counting."

Owen chuckled. "I thought even you could count up to two."

"I've scored loads more than that."

"In friendly games maybe, but I'm talking about Sunday League matches," Owen said.

"You haven't found the net for three weeks."

"How do *you* know?" Jake snapped. "You don't come to the games."

"I've checked in your little black book."

"That's private!" cried Jake.

He didn't think Owen knew about the soccer diary he kept in his bedside cabinet. "I'm going to—"

"You've got a bite!" Owen yelled. "Strike!"

Jake saw the float bobbing and he struck. He felt a slight tug on the line but then the fish was gone – and so was another worm.

"That was *your* fault," he said

bitterly, staring at the bare
hook.

"Another one that got away,"
Owen giggled. "Just like all
those chances last Sunday."

"Who said that?"

"Adam."

Chapter Two
Off Target

"Take your time, Jake. Don't snatch at it."

That might have been a good piece of advice to help him catch a fish, but this comment came from the Rangers' team manager.

It was the squad's Thursday evening training session in the sports hall and the strikers were having extra shooting practice.

Jake clearly needed it. His latest shot bounced off the wall and almost hit the goalkeeper on the back of the head.

"Huh! That would have gone right in the top corner in a proper goal," Jake moaned. "This one is too small."

"No excuses, Jake," Mr Burrows told him. "And there are no prizes for breaking the net either. You're trying to hit the ball too hard."

"I know how to score goals," he replied cheekily, only just stopping himself from using the manager's nickname of Rabbit.

"I *was* Rangers' top scorer last season, remember."

"Yes, but it's *this* season I'm interested in now," Mr Burrows said, curling his top lip to reveal the twin prongs of his two buck-teeth.

"One-season wonder," mocked Sameer, the goalkeeper. "We've had two school matches this term and Jake hasn't scored in either of them."

Jake glared at him. "It's not worth the bother," he retorted. "Not when you keep letting goals in at our end."

"Come on, lads, it's no good getting at each other," said Mr Burrows. "We need teamwork on Sunday to beat Villa."

The manager knew how keen his players were to do that. A win for Rangers would see them leapfrog over their local rivals in the league table.

	P	W	D	L	F	A	Pts
VILLA	8	6	1	1	24	5	19
RANGERS	8	6	0	2	22	7	18
PARK	8	5	1	2	18	4	16
ROVERS	8	4	2	2	18	8	14
SOUTH	8	4	1	3	12	7	13
UNITED	8	3	0	5	10	14	9
JSB	8	1	3	4	6	22	6
SUTTON	8	1	1	6	3	30	4

"Yeah, I'm fed up with the Villa lot at school bragging about how they beat us twice last season," Jake said and then

20

took the chance to do a bit of
boasting himself. "So I'm going
to shut them up by scoring a
hat–trick!"

Mr Burrows chuckled. "Well,
if you do that,
Jake, you can
keep the
match
ball," he
promised.

"Wicked!"
cried Jake.

Adam let his feet do the
talking. When it was his turn
to shoot, he showed everybody

how to do it. He flicked the
ball up into the air with his
right foot and, as the ball
dropped, he lashed a left-footed
volley past Sameer.

"Great goal, Adam!"

The shout came from the top of the wall-bars lining one side of the hall where Owen was watching. He had turned up in the hope that Rabbit might let him join in if they were a player short.

"Bet you can't beat that, Jake," Owen taunted.

Jake didn't even try. His next shot went nowhere near the goal – deliberately. He had another target in his sights – his little brother.

It was just as well for Owen that Jake's shooting was so wild. The ball crashed into the wall-bars two metres from his head, but the shock of its impact almost made Owen fall off his perch.

"Watch it, Jake!" warned
Adam. "That was a pretty
stupid thing to do."

Mr Burrows agreed. He let
Owen take his brother's place
in the practice game that
followed and made Jake sit at
the side instead.

"Huh! You wait till Sunday,
Rabbit," Jake muttered under
his breath. "I'm going to have
that match ball!"

Chapter Three

Promise

"Look at that one!" Jake cried, pointing into the brook. "What a beauty!"

"Where?" demanded Adam. "I can't see it."

"Too late now. It's gone."

"I bet it was never there in the first place."

"Would I lie to you?"

"I thought every fisherman lied," Adam said. "You know, about how many they catch."

"I don't."

"So how many do you usually catch?"

"Oh, loads!" Jake grinned, unable to keep a straight face.

Jake and his friend had spent
most of Saturday
afternoon
kicking an old
ball about in
the park. When
the ball burst, they
had wandered along the
water's edge until they came to
a loop in the brook.
It formed a deep
pool where the
fish could lie
hidden and wait
for food to be
washed downstream to them.

...aught my biggest-ever fish
...e," Jake claimed.

"Yeah, so you've said," Adam
sighed, hoping not to hear the
story again. "Surprised you
didn't bring your rod with you
today."

"Mum wouldn't let me," Jake admitted. "Just because she found my tin of maggots in

the fridge! She went totally bananas!"

Adam's laughter made Jake change the subject.

"Do you think Rabbit would really give me the match ball?" he asked.

"How should I know?"

"Yeah, but what do you *think*? You know, honestly."

Adam paused for a moment. "*Honestly*? You mean, like a fisherman?"

Jake pulled a face at his friend.

"Well, OK, then," Adam said, tossing a stick into the current to watch it float away. "No."

"What do you mean – *no*?" demanded Jake. "He promised."

"Only because he knows you won't score a hat-trick. Not against Villa."

"I might."

Adam shrugged. "Well, maybe – if you have some help from me," he said as an idea popped into his head. "But it will cost you."

"How much?"

"I'm not talking about money."

"What, then? Do you want to share the ball?"

"No, you can keep the ball," Adam smiled. "I just want a promise from you too."

"Name it."

"Well," Adam began, "I'll do everything I can tomorrow to help you get a hat-trick if—"

"What about penalties?" Jake cut in, knowing how Adam always insisted on taking them himself to boost his own goal tally.

To Jake's surprise, Adam simply nodded and went on, ". . . but only if you promise to give up fishing!"

Chapter Four
Football or Fishing?

"Goal!" Jake screamed.

The match could not have started better for Rangers – or for Jake. His very first touch of the ball sent it skidding past the Villa keeper into the net.

Jake celebrated by flinging
himself full-length across the
wet grass as if diving into the
brook. Adam joined in and
landed heavily on top of him.

"Magic!" Adam cried. "Now
that's what I call an early
strike!"

"One down, two to go," shouted Owen from the  touchline. He knew about their deal and had been unable to resist coming to watch what happened.

Jake and Adam picked themselves up and jogged back towards the centre-circle together.

"I wonder if old Rabbit wants me to score a hat-trick or not," Jake said.

"I don't know," replied Adam, "but I sure do."

Jake glanced across towards the brook. "Yeah, but do *I* really want to?" he sighed.

Given such a wonderful start,
Rangers were full of
confidence. They might easily
have added to their lead, but
they wasted several good
chances. Both Jake and Adam
sent shots wide from close
range.

By half-time, however, Villa had battled their way back into the match. The Rangers' goalie Sameer made two smart saves but he was well beaten by a header from a corner.

"You've only got yourselves to blame," the manager told his players during the short break. "You can't afford to let a side like Villa off the hook . . ."

Jake didn't hear much more of what was said. Mention of the word *hook* only made him think of fishing again. He was already beginning to regret making that promise to Adam.

"Are you listening to me, Jake?"

Hearing his name jolted Jake's attention back into gear. He realized everybody was looking at him and sniggering.

"I thought not," fumed Mr Burrows. "If I didn't know you better, I might have believed you missed that open goal on purpose. Even Owen could have scored from there."

Owen was standing behind
the manager, making rabbit
faces by sticking his front teeth
out. He didn't think
that last remark
was meant as a
compliment.
As the boys
finished their
half-time
slices of
orange, Owen
sidled up to his
older brother. "Well?"
he began. "Are you trying to
score that hat-trick or not?"

Jake gave a shrug. "You can't score a goal every time you shoot, you know. Just like you can't catch a fish every time you strike."

"*You* can't, anyway," Owen said cheekily. He then produced Jake's soccer diary from his coat pocket.

"What are you doing with that?" Jake stormed. "Give it here."

Owen skipped away, knowing Jake couldn't chase after him. The referee was waiting to restart the game.

"If you want it back, you know what you have to do," Owen taunted, waving the diary in the air. "No hat-trick, no book. I'll throw it into the water to feed the fishes!"

Chapter Five

Penalty!

As the second half began, so did the rain, which didn't improve Jake's mood. Two wild tackles earned him a warning from the referee.

"Cool it, Jake," Adam told him. "No good getting yourself sent off – at least not till you've grabbed a couple more goals."

The next goal, however, went to Villa. Sameer spoiled his previous good work by letting a shot slither through his hands – and through his legs. Villa were 2–1 ahead.

"Come on, Rangers," yelled Mr Burrows. "Get a grip."

In the wet conditions, it wasn't easy for anyone to follow that kind of advice. All the players were struggling to keep on their feet when they tried to turn or run with the ball.

The Villa captain tried to show off by dribbling the ball out of defence, but he didn't get very far. The ball got stuck in a puddle, the captain slipped over and Jake pounced.

Five seconds later, the ball was on its way into the Villa net. Jake had found his shooting boots at last.

The ball dipped and swerved, leaving the goalkeeper helpless.

It looked as if the Villa team settled for a draw after that. They pulled extra players back into defence and wasted time by kicking the ball anywhere upfield or out of play.

Sameer could almost have leant on one of his goalposts underneath an umbrella.

The match moved into its closing stages with the teams still level at 2–2. The vital third goal Jake needed for his hat-trick just would not come.

"Oh, well," he sighed. "At least I'll still be able to go fishing . . ."

"Penalty!"

The only Rangers player who didn't join in the loud appeal was Adam. He was still lying face down in the goalmouth mud after being fouled.

As the referee pointed to the penalty spot, Jake helped Adam back up onto his feet.

"I'm taking it, remember,"
Jake insisted.

Adam spat out some mud.
"Are you sure?"

Jake nodded.

"You know what it means if
you score? No more fishing."

Jake took a deep breath. "I
know," he said simply and

picked up the ball.

"What do you
think you're doing,
Jake?" Mr Burrows
bellowed across the
pitch. "You take it,
Adam."

"But Jake's on a hat-trick,"
Adam called out.

"Never mind that. Winning
this match is more important!"
The two friends looked at
each other.

"I guess he
doesn't
want me
to have
the ball,"
Jake
muttered.
"Maybe
not," Adam replied and then he
winked. "But I do."

The referee lost his patience. "Hurry up, Rangers. Get on with it."

By this time, Owen had run round the pitch to position himself behind the goal. He had Jake's record book in his hand and mimed the action of throwing it away.

"Don't you dare," Jake snarled. "It's not my fault, you know. You heard what old Rabbit just said."

Jake went to stand with the other players outside the penalty area as Adam placed the ball on the muddy penalty spot.

"Get ready," he called to Jake.

"What for?"

"Ready to strike!"

Peeeeeppp!!!

The referee still had the whistle in his mouth as Adam ran in and blasted the ball dead straight. The goalkeeper was so surprised that all he could do was parry the ball in self-defence. It was too hot to handle.

The ball bounced back towards Adam who stepped aside to allow his teammate more room. Jake reacted quickly and he swept the ball home to clinch Rangers a 3–2 victory.

At the final whistle, Owen
ran onto the pitch to give Jake
his book.

"Here you
are," he
laughed.
"Plenty of
room left
in it to
write all
about your
hat-trick."

Having already grabbed the
match ball, Jake snatched the
book from his brother. "I'll get
you later for nicking this."

"Let him off," said Adam,
draping an arm around Owen's
shoulders. "He was only
helping me to save the fish."

"Huh! He needn't have bothered," Jake replied before making a confession. "I hardly ever caught anything, anyway. I'd rather put a ball in the net than a fish."

"That's what I like to hear," Adam laughed. "But you sure left it late."

"Yeah, well, it's all a matter of timing," Jake grinned. "Better late than never!"

THE END